Junie B. Jones
and the
Mushy Gushy
Valentime

by Barbara Park
illustrated by Denise Brunkus

A STEPPING STONE BOOK™

Random House 🏠 New York

Text copyright © 1999 by Barbara Park
Illustrations copyright © 1999 by Denise Brunkus
All rights reserved under International and Pan-American Copyright
Conventions. Published in the United States by Random House, Inc.,
and simultaneously in Canada by Random House of Canada Limited,
Toronto.

www.randomhouse.com/kids/junieb

Library of Congress Cataloging-in-Publication Data

Park, Barbara.
Junie B. Jones and the mushy gushy valentime [i.e. valentine] /
by Barbara Park ; illustrated by Denise Brunkus.
   p.   cm. "A stepping stone book."
SUMMARY: When Junie B. Jones receives a mushy gushy "valentime"
on Valentine's Day, she tries to find out who in her kindergarten class
is her secret admirer.
ISBN 0-375-80039-5 (trade) — ISBN 0-375-90039-X (lib. bdg.)
[1. Valentine's Day—Fiction.   2. Valentines—Fiction.
3. Kindergarten—Fiction.   4. Schools—Fiction.]
I. Brunkus, Denise, ill.   II. Title.
PZ7.P2197Jtslm   1999   [Fic]—dc21   99-40615

Printed in the United States of America December 1999 **20 19 18 17 16**

A STEPPING STONE BOOK and colophon are trademarks of Random House, Inc.

Contents

1/ Party Ideas

My name is Junie B. Jones. The B stands for Beatrice. Except I don't like Beatrice. I just like B and that's all.

I go to school in Room Nine. Room Nine is where they have afternoon kindergarten.

Also they have morning kindergarten. Only I am not familiar with that arrangement.

Today at school, my teacher had a 'nouncement to make.

A *'nouncement* is the school word for *listen to me...and I MEAN it.*

My teacher's name is Mrs. She has another name, too. But I just like Mrs. and that's all.

Mrs. told us that we are going to have a special day in Room Nine. And it is called Valentime's Day.

She said that valentimes are special cards about friendship. And all of us in Room Nine are going to give them to each other!

My bestest friend Lucille squealed real happy.

"Oooo! I love getting cards, Teacher!" she said. "I especially love getting the kind with money in them. Money is my favorite kind of mail!"

"Me, too, Lucille!" I said. "Money is my favorite kind of mail, too. Plus also I enjoy the Publishers Clearing House sweepstakes."

Mrs. did a chuckle.

"Well, I'm sorry, girls. But I'm afraid there won't be money in our valentines," she said. "In Room Nine we will just be sending happy wishes to each other. But it will still be lots of fun."

She smiled.

"We will be making a special valentines box to hold all the cards. And on the day of our party, I will personally deliver the cards to each one of you," she explained.

Just then, I jumped right out of my chair. 'Cause nobody even mentioned a party before!

"Hurray!" I yelled. "Hurray for parties! Can we have cake and doughnuts, Mrs.? And what about cheese popcorn and cotton candy and pretzels and candy apples?"

I thought some more.

"Plus also we'll need red licorice

and peanut butter cups, probably. And chocolate-covered raisins. Oh yeah, and malted milk balls! AND GUMMI BEARS!"

I looked over at her.

"Maybe you should be writing this down," I said.

Mrs. shook her head no. She said we would have cupcakes, punch, and candy hearts.

I sat back down very disappointed.

'Cause not much thought went into the menu, that's why.

Lucille stood up.

"What kind of punch, Teacher?" she asked. "Will it have fresh raspberries and strawberries floating in it? My nanna's caterer always puts fresh raspberries and strawberries into our punch. And it is delicious."

After that, Lucille twirled around in her fluffy dress.

"And what about dancing? I am learning ballroom dancing at my expensive dancing school. And so I would be happy to teach the children who are cheaper than me."

Mrs. stared at Lucille a real long time.

"How very generous of you," she said finally. "But I don't think we'll be having ballroom dancing, Lucille."

Jamal Hall waved his hand in the air.

"Then what about a puppet show?" he asked. "If we can't have dancing, can we have a puppet show?"

"Yes," said a girl named Lynnie. "Or else maybe we could hire a magician."

"Or what about a wild animal act?" asked a boy named Roger. "Like a grizzly bear or a sea lion?"

Just then, a boy named Paulie Allen Puffer ran right to the front of the room. And he jumped up and down all over the place.

"NO! WAIT! I'VE GOT IT! I'VE GOT IT!" he shouted real excited. "WE COULD GET SOME OF THOSE JUGGLERS WHO JUGGLE CHAIN SAWS!"

After that, Room Nine clapped and whistled and hooted and hollered.

'Cause who doesn't love chain-saw jugglers? That's what I would like to know!

After we finished clapping, we looked at Mrs.

Her head was on her desk. And her eyes were staring out the door.

Then all of the children in Room Nine got very quiet.

'Cause Mrs. was scaring us a little bit.

Plus also we were out of party ideas.

2/ Scribble Scraps

The next day, me and my bestest friend named Grace were playing on the playground.

And guess what?

We saw Mrs. carry a giant box into Room Nine!

It was the box we were going to decorate for Valentime's Day, I think!

"Wowie wow wow! That thing will hold a million bajillion Valentime's cards!" I said real thrilled.

That Grace did a frown at me.

"Stop saying valen*time*, Junie B.," she said. "You keep on saying valen*time* with an *m* sound. And you are supposed to say valen*tine* with an *n* sound."

I did a frown back at her.

"Who said so?" I asked.

"I said so," said that Grace. "Didn't you hear my voice? I just got finished telling you it has an *n* in it. The word is valen*tine*."

I did a huffy breath at that girl.

"You are not the boss of my words, Grace," I said. "This is a freed country. And if I want to say valen*time*, I can. And I will not even go to jail."

That Grace looked annoyed at me.

"I didn't *say* you would go to jail, Junie B.," she said. "I just wish you would say the word correctly, that's all."

"Yeah well, we can't always have what we wish for, Grace," I told her. "I wish valentime had an m in it. But it doesn't, does it?"

After that, me and that Grace made squinty eyes at each other. Plus also we crossed our arms. And we tapped our angry feet.

Only pretty soon we got tired of that. 'Cause fighting with your friends is not that fun.

That's how come both of us hugged each other. And we said a 'pology.

"Sorry, Junie B.," said Grace. "Sorry I tried to be the boss of your words."

"Sorry, Grace," I said back. "Sorry valentime doesn't have an m in it."

After that, both of us holded hands. And we skipped all the way to Room Nine.

That is called a victory skip.

And guess what else?

After we got to Room Nine, Mrs. said it was time to decorate the valentimes box!

Everybody quick sat down in their seats.

Then we watched Mrs. cover the box with shiny white paper. Plus also she cut a mail slot in the top.

After that, all of the children got our scissors. And we cut out paper hearts to paste onto the sides.

I cut my fastest.

"Mrs.! Look! Look!" I said. "I am already done cutting my heart! And so I have the fastest scissors in Room Nine, probably!"

Just then, a meanie boy named Jim jumped up from his chair.

"No, you don't! Look over here! I already cut *two* hearts! See? One...two! So ha ha on you!" he said.

I quick cut another heart.

"Yeah, well now I have two, too! And so you are not the winner anymore, Meanie Jim!"

Jim held up one more.

"Three!" he yelled. "I just cut number

three! So I am still one ahead of you!"

I made my scissors go speedy fast.

"Ha! Now I have three, too. So there!" I said.

Jim did a fast snip.

"Four! I'm up to four!" he said.

That's how come I got fusstration inside me.

"STOP IT, JIM! STOP CUTTING SO FAST! AND I MEAN IT!"

After that, I tried to cut one more heart. But my scissors went very out of control. And my heart turned out like scribble scraps!

"DARN IT! *NOW* LOOK WHAT YOU MADE ME DO!" I hollered real mad.

All of a sudden, a big hand came flying over the top of my head. And it snatched my scissors right off my fingers.

I bended my head back to see who it was.

It was Mrs.

I did a gulp.

"I was afraid it was you," I said kind of soft.

Then Mrs. went to Jim's table. And she snatched his scissors, too.

And so me and him had to sit in our chairs for the rest of the day. And we didn't get to decorate the valentimes box.

'Cause our cutting days were over, that's why.

And our pasting days never even got started.

3/

Picking Out Valentimes!

The valentimes box turned out very beautiful!

After it was finished, Mrs. passed out lists for us to take home. The lists had the names of all the children in Room Nine.

"There are eighteen children in our class," said Mrs. "So that means that everyone needs to bring eighteen valentines."

I raised my hand.

"Do we bring valentimes for ourselves, too?" I asked her.

"Well, no," she said. "I mean there's no rule against it, I suppose. But valentines are really supposed to be given to others."

She thought for a second.

"Oops. I guess that means I made a mistake, doesn't it?" she said. "Since you won't be bringing in cards for yourselves, you will only need to bring in seventeen valentines."

I raised up my hand again.

"Yeah, only what if we also want to bring a valentime for *you*, Mrs.?" I asked.

Mrs. raised up her eyebrows.

"Well, then you would be back up to eighteen again. Wouldn't you?" she said. "Seventeen plus one equals eighteen."

I tapped on my chin.

"Yeah, only what if there's people in here

who we don't actually like that much? Do we have to bring them a valentime, too?"

"Yes, Junie B.," she said. "Of course you do. Valentine's Day is a day of friendship for *everyone*. So every single boy and girl in Room Nine will bring a card for every other boy and girl."

After Mrs. finished explaining, she sat back down at her desk.

I zoomed up there and whispered in her ear.

"Yeah, only I know I have to bring cards to the *regular* boys and girls," I said real soft. "But I don't have to bring cards to the big, fat stinky heads, do I?"

All of a sudden, Mrs. throwed her arms in the air.

"Yes, Junie B.! Yes, you do!" she said. "For the last time…you will bring a card for

everyone in Room Nine. Even the big, fat stinky heads!"

Just then, all of Room Nine looked at her.

'Cause teachers are not supposed to say *big, fat stinky heads,* I think.

After that, Mrs. closed her eyes for a real long time.

Then finally, she stood up very slow.

And she went to the sink.

And she took aspirin.

The next day was Saturday.

And it was the funnest Saturday ever!

'Cause Daddy took me to the drugstore! And he bought me beautiful heart antennas for my head! Plus also he let me pick out my very own box of valentimes!

After we got home, Mother helped me pick out the perfect cards for every person in Room Nine.

First, I picked a card for my bestest friend Lucille. It had a lovely princess on the front of it.

"This one, Mother!" I said. "I will give

Lucille this one! 'Cause when she grows up, she is going to marry an expensive prince! And she is going to let me and Grace sweep her castle! Plus also we will get to wear her raggedy used-up gowns!"

Mother looked and looked at me.

"Lucille is a regular saint," she said very quiet.

"I know it," I said. "Me and Grace are lucky to have her."

After that, I found the perfect card for Grace, too. It had two running shoes on the front of it!

Mother read me the words.

It said, *Valentine! You and I make the perfect pair!*

"We do, Mother! Me and that Grace do make the perfect pair! 'Cause Grace can beat me at running! And I can beat Grace at lots of other stuff, probably! Only I haven't actually found anything yet."

After that, I picked out special cards for all of the other children in Room Nine.

Every time I picked out a valentime, Mother crossed a name off the list.

Finally, there was only one name left.

"Jim," said Mother. "You still need to pick a card for Jim."

I did a big sigh. 'Cause I didn't want to give that guy one, of course.

I looked all through my box of valentimes.

Then, all of a sudden, I saw a card with a funny skunk on the front.

"That one," I said. "I will send Jim that one."

Mother shook her head.

"I don't know, Junie B.," she said. "A

22

picture of a skunk just doesn't seem very nice."

I put it in an envelope.

"Perfect," I said. "'Cause neither is Jim."

4/ The Disagreedment

On Monday I skipped into Room Nine very thrilled.

"Mrs.! Mrs.! Look!" I said. "I have all my valentimes for the big, giant valentimes box! They are right here in this paper bag I am carrying!"

I runned and showed her inside it.

"See them? See them, Mrs.? I matched every single card to the exact person who will get it!" I explained.

Mrs. patted my head. She said the word *good job*.

Then she took me by my hand. And she showed me how to put my valentimes through the mail slot in the box.

"I do believe that you are the very first person in Room Nine to bring in her cards," said Mrs.

I did a gasp at that exciting news!

"*First,* Mrs.?" I asked. "I am really, really first?"

After that, I springed way high in the air. And I ran around and around in a circle.

"I've never been first at anything before!" I said real squealy. "Not ever, ever never! And so what is my prize for winning?"

I closed my eyes and held out my hands.

"Put it right in my hands, okay, Mrs.? I won't even peek. I promise!"

After that, I stood there real patient. But

nothing got put in my hands.

Finally, Mrs. bended down next to my ear.

"Junie B., honey, I'm really sorry. But there is no prize," she said. "We weren't actually having a contest."

I opened my eyes.

"We weren't?" I asked.

Mrs. shook her head no.

My shoulders slumped a teeny bit.

"So then, a prize would be out of the question, probably," I said.

Mrs. shrugged. "I'm afraid I didn't buy any prizes," she said.

After that, I rocked back and forth on my feet. And I thought and thought.

"Would you have a mint in your drawer, maybe? Or some stickers?" I asked.

Mrs. smiled.

Then she took me to her desk. And we looked in her drawer.

"How about a broken piece of chalk and a yellow rubber band?" she asked.

"Sold!" I said.

After that, Mrs. told me congratulations. And she gave me my prizes.

I quick skipped to my table to show them to Lucille.

She wrinkled up her nose.

"Yuck. Have you been going through the trash can again?" she asked.

"No, silly! These are my prizes!" I said. "I got prizes for bringing in my valentimes first!"

Lucille smoothed her dress.

"Yes, well, I would have brought my cards in today, too. But they're not back from the printers yet," she told me.

"What?" I said. "What printers?"

"The printers where they print my name on the cards," she said. "Wait till you see them, Junie B.! Every card will have *Love and kisses from Lucille* on the bottom of it!"

She hugged herself.

"They are so beautiful," she said. "Each valentine has a cherry lollipop on the front. And the lollipop is in the shape of Cupid."

She sighed very dreamy.

"Cupid is the symbol of Valentine's Day, you know," she said.

"Of course I know," I said back. "Plus also skunks and shoes are symbols of Valentime's Day, too. 'Cause that's what are on my cards."

After that, me and Lucille did our work till recess.

Then both of us went outside to play with our other bestest friend, Grace.

Only too bad for us. 'Cause Lucille kept on bragging about Valentime's Day. And that's how come she and that Grace got into a disagreedment.

"I am going to get more valentines than anyone," bragged Lucille. "That's because the boys love me better than any other girl. And they will bring me lots and lots of cards."

Grace looked curious at her.

"But Mrs. said to only bring one card for every boy and girl, remember? Not lots and lots."

Lucille flounced her flouncy dress.

"Silly Grace. Look at me, for goodness' sake! I am precious! And when you're precious, boys automatically bring you lots of valentines. They just can't help theirselves."

She twirled all around.

"I am the cutest girl in Room Nine, Grace," she said. "I am way cuter than anyone else."

She giggled and pointed. "Even you."

After that, Grace did a little frown. 'Cause that hurt her feelings, I think.

I tapped on Lucille.

"Yeah, only Grace is the nicest, Lucille,"

I said. "And so maybe the boys will bring her lots of valentimes, too."

Lucille did a huffy breath at me.

"But I'm *richer* than Grace, Junie B. So that is another reason to bring me more," she said.

I thought for a minute.

"Yes, but Grace can run faster," I said.

"So?" said Lucille. "My hair is longer. And boys like long hair."

I looked at Grace's head.

"But Grace's hair is springier and curlier," I said. "And that is cute as a button."

Lucille made squinty eyes at me.

"But I have a big-screen TV. And a pool!" she said real loud.

That's how come me and that Grace leaned our heads together. And we got in a huggle.

Finally, I looked up at Lucille.

"Okay. Here's what we came up with," I said. "Grace can whistle through her teeth. Plus she can wiggle her ears. And also, she can dribble a basketball through her legs while she's running."

Lucille jumped up and down.

"BUT I HAVE A PONY!" she hollered.

I patted her very sympathetic.

"Sorry," I said real soft. "Grace has a *snake*."

After that, Lucille's shoulders got very sagging. And she sat down in the grass.

'Cause boys love snakes better than anything.

Pretty soon, that Grace sat down next to Lucille. And she put her arm around Lucille's shoulders. And she patted her.

'Cause guess what else?

Grace is a good sport.

5/ Valentime's Time

Valentime's Day came on Friday!

And guess what? My grandma Helen Miller bought me a special Valentime's outfit! And it matched my heart antennas very perfect!

That day at school, I skipped all around Room Nine. 'Cause I was a treat for the eyes, I tell you!

Finally, I sat in my seat. And Mrs. took attendance.

And guess what? Nobody was absent!

'Cause who wants to miss a party, that's why!

After attendance, Mrs. put on a special Valentime's apron. It had a big heart pocket in the front.

Then Mrs. filled the heart pocket with Valentime's cards from the box. And she delivered them to all of the children.

And wait till you hear this!

The very first valentime was delivered to me! To Junie B. Jones! And it said my name right on the envelope!

"YAHOO!" I shouted real thrilled. "I AM FIRST *AGAIN*, MRS.! YAHOO! YAHOO!"

After that, Mrs. kept on delivering cards until the whole valentimes box was empty.

Then all of us got to open up our cards. And it was as fun as a birthday party, I tell you!

After Lucille finished opening her valen-times, she called Grace to our table.

"Come here, Grace! Come here and bring your valentines! Then you and I can count our cards. And we'll see who got the most from the boys," she said.

Grace came over.

She smiled kind of nervous.

"Well…okay. Here goes," she said.

Then Grace put all of her valentimes in front of me and Lucille. And she counted them one by one.

Pretty soon, Grace wasn't smiling any-more.

"Rats. I knew I shouldn't have come over here," she said.

Lucille grinned a teeny bit.

"Why, Grace?" she asked. "How many did you get? You have to tell me, Grace. How many?"

Grace did a big sigh.

"I only got seventeen," she said. "I only got one card from every person. And that's all. No extras."

Lucille's face lighted up very bright. She flipped her hair all around in the air.

"Gee, I am sorry to hear that, Grace," she said. "Well, I suppose I should count mine now."

After that, Lucille counted her cards in front of me and Grace. She counted them right out loud.

"Thirteen…fourteen…fifteen…sixteen…"

All of a sudden, Lucille stopped counting. 'Cause there was only one more valentime left in her pile, that's why.

She quick stood up at her seat. And looked all around herself.

First, she looked under the table. Then she looked on top of her chair. And all over the floor.

Also she looked in her pockets. And her backpack. And her purse.

Finally, she sat back down real upset.

"I don't understand," she said. "How

could this be happening? Every day my nanna tells me how special I am. But seventeen valentines isn't special at all. Seventeen valentines is just the same as everybody else."

I did a sigh.

"Nannas," I said. "You can't believe a word they say."

Grace looked cheerier.

"Count yours, Junie B. Count your valentines and see if you got seventeen like Lucille and me."

"Of course I got seventeen, silly Grace," I told her. "Everybody in this whole room got seventeen. It was the rule, remember?"

After that, I put all my cards in a pile. And I counted them out loud, just like Lucille.

I did a frown.

Then I counted them again.

And even again.

'Cause guess what?

Somebody broke the rule, that's what!

I springed up on my chair.

"ALL RIGHT, PEOPLE! WHO DIDN'T SEND ME A VALENTIME? AND DO NOT TRY TO DENY IT! BECAUSE I'VE ONLY GOT SIXTEEN CARDS IN MY PILE!"

I pointed my finger at Meanie Jim.

"WAS IT *YOU*, MISTER? HUH? ARE YOU THE MEANIE HEAD WHO DIDN'T SEND ME ONE?"

I looked all around.

"OR MAYBE IT WAS *YOU*, MR. PAULIE ALLEN PUFFER...

"OR *YOU*, CHARLOTTE WHO-I-DON'T-ACTUALLY-KNOW-YOUR-LAST-NAME...

"OR *YOU*, ROGER...

"OR—"

Just then, Mrs. swooped me off my chair.

"Do *not* stand on your chair, Junie B.!" she said. "And please don't fight about valentines. If someone didn't send you a card, it was just a mistake. No one would do something like that on purpose. I'm sure of it."

After that, I sat back down in my seat. And I looked at that woman very curious.

Because Mrs. is a nice teacher.

But sometimes she doesn't understand children at all.

6/ Bingo

I put my head down on my table. 'Cause I needed to figure out who didn't send me a valentime, that's why.

I thinked and thinked real hard.

Then, all of a sudden, I springed up.

"Lucille! I thinked of a plan! I thinked of how to find that guy! All I have to do is see the names of who signed my valentimes! 'Cause whoever is missing is the person who didn't send me one!"

Lucille looked admiring at me.

"That is very smart of you, Junie B.," she said. "You should be on *Cops*."

"I know it," I said back. "My head is as sharp as a tack."

After that, I got all of my valentimes in a pile. And me and Lucille looked at the people who signed them.

We kept track of their names very good.

Only too bad for me. 'Cause seven of my valentimes weren't even signed!

"Darn it," I said. "*Now* what am I supposed to do?"

Just then, I saw Mrs. hurrying to my table again.

"Junie B.? I have some good news for you!" she said. "Guess what I just found in the bottom of the valentines box?"

I sat up real quick.

'Cause guessing games are my favorites, of course.

"A meatball," I said.

Mrs. did a frown.

"No, Junie B. Why would there be a meatball in the box? Think about it. What have people been putting in the valentines box all week?"

"Valentime's cards," I said real smart.

"Right," she said. "And how many valentines did you get today?"

"Sixteen," I told her.

"Yes," she said. "You were missing one, weren't you? And so what do you think I found in the bottom of the box just now?"

This time I thought my hardest.

"A meatball," I said.

45

Mrs. rolled her eyes up at the ceiling. Then I looked up there, too. But I didn't see anything.

Finally, Mrs. pulled a giant envelope from behind her back.

"No, *this,* Junie B.," she said. "*This* is what I found in the bottom of the box. I found this big envelope. And it's addressed to *you!*"

My mouth came open very shocked.

Then all of a sudden, I clapped my hands very thrilled.

"HEY! WAIT A SECOND HERE! MAYBE THIS COULD BE MY MISSING VALENTIME!"

Mrs. looked funny at me. "Bingo," she said kind of soft.

"YES!" I shouted. "BINGO! BINGO! BINGO!"

After that, I jumped up and down. And I danced all around. 'Cause nobody broke the rule after all! And that was very nice of them!

After I finished dancing, I opened up the envelope.

And it was the beautifullest card I ever saw!

It had lace and hearts all over the front! And a purple ribbon was weaved all around the edge!

"Look, Mrs.! Look! Look! It's a mushy gushy kind!" I said. "I always wanted one of these things! Who sent it? Huh? Read me their name, okay? Who sent it? Who sent it?"

Mrs. opened up the card and looked at the name.

Then she laughed out loud.

"Well, well, well...it looks like you've got yourself a fan," she said.

She ruffled my hair.

"This card is signed, *From Your Secret Admirer*."

I raised up my eyebrows.

"Huh? What? Who?"

Mrs. smiled.

"A secret admirer is someone who likes you very much, but he's too shy to tell you," she explained.

"I guess your Valentine's Day turned out pretty good after all, huh?" she said.

"Yes! My Valentime's Day turned out almost perfect!" I said. "Now all I have to do is figure out who my secret admirer is, and I will be in business!"

After that, I put my head on my table. And I closed my eyes.

'Cause I needed to think of another plan, of course!

7 / Wink, Wink

Another plan did not come easy.

I thinked and thinked for a real long time.

Finally, I tapped on my bestest friend Lucille.

"Want to help me, Lucille?" I asked. "Want to help me figure out my secret admirer?"

Lucille did mad eyes at me.

"Just because you have a secret admirer doesn't mean you're prettier than me," she said very annoyed.

I looked surprised at her.

"I never said I was prettier, Lucille," I said. "It's just that someone in Room Nine loves me better than he loves you. And I keep on wondering who it is."

Lucille leaned close to my face.

"It's a cuckoo head boy, that's who it is," she said.

After that, she scooted her chair to the end of the table. And she turned her head away from me.

I did a mad breath at that girl.

"Keep acting like that, and you'll be sweeping your own castle," I said.

After that, I looked all around Room Nine.

And guess who I saw?

I saw Crybaby William, that's who!

Crybaby William sits right behind me.

And is the shyest guy I ever heard of. And so maybe *he* might be my secret admirer!

I spinned around in my chair and waved at him.

"Hello, shy boy," I said real cute.

William looked nervous of me. "What do you want?" he said.

I wrinkled up my nose very darling.

"Yeah, only you don't even have to be shy of me anymore, William. 'Cause I think I know your secret," I said.

After that, I put my chin on his table. And I winked my eye at him. Only I'm not actually good at winking. And so I have to say the words.

"Wink, wink, William," I said. "Wink, wink, wink. See my eye? See how it is trying to wink at you?"

William's face started to sweat.

"Turn around, please," he said.

I did a giggle. 'Cause that admirer boy was shyer than I thought.

"You are a silly sausage, William," I said.

Then I tried to tickle him under his chin. But William swatted my hand away.

I tapped my fingers on the table.

"Okay. Here's the thing, William. Swatting my hand is not actually that admiring. And so please do not do that again."

After that, I tried to tickle his chin again. But this time, he ducked under the table.

I did a frown.

'Cause something did not seem right here.

Finally, I bended my head down and I peeked at him.

"I'm going to take a wild guess here, William. You're not actually my secret admirer, are you?" I asked.

"No!" said William. "No, no, no!"

After that, I did a big sigh. And I turned my chair back to my own table.

I looked all around Room Nine again.

And guess what boy I saw next?

I saw Paulie Allen Puffer, that's who! And he is always teasing me! And so maybe *he* is my secret admirer!

I zoomed to his table speedy fast.

"Wink, wink, Paulie Allen Puffer," I said. "Wink, wink, wink."

"What's wrong with your eye?" he said.

I puckered up my lips. And I blowed that guy a kiss.

"Thank you for the beautiful valentime, Paul," I said.

Paulie Allen Puffer looked strange at me.

"Paul? Who's Paul? What beautiful valentine? My valentine was the one with the oozy slime monster on the front," he said. "Don't you remember it?"

Just then, I made a face. 'Cause I remembered it, of course.

I hurried up back to my seat again.

That's when I saw a boy named Ham. And Ham hardly even *knows* me. And so he was worth a try, I think.

I quick went to his table.

"Okay, Ham. I'm running out of patience here. So listen very careful."

I faced my eyeball at him.

"Wink, wink, okay? Now are you my secret admirer or not? And please tell me the truth. Or you will be sorry. "

Ham sticked out his tongue at me.

Also he put his thumbs in his ears. And he flapped his hands up and down.

"All rightie," I said. "I'm going to take that as a no."

After that, I went back to my table. And I sat down real fusstrated.

I put my head in my hands very glum.

'Cause guess what?

Finding a secret admirer is not as easy as it sounds.

8/ Who Knew?

Pretty soon, the bell rang for recess.

I hurried over to my friend Grace. 'Cause maybe *she* would help me find my secret admirer.

Both of us skipped outside to the playground.

Then all of a sudden, I stopped real fast! 'Cause I accidentally left my beautiful valentime on the table! And I didn't want anyone to take that lovely thing!

"Wait, Grace! Wait right here! I will be back in a jiffy!" I said.

After that, I ran my fastest back to Room Nine.

And guess what?

I spied that Meanie Jim at my table!

And he was picking up my beautiful card!

"HEY! WHAT DO YOU THINK YOU ARE DOING, MISTER?" I yelled real loud.

Then I zoomed to my table zippedy quick. And I yanked that card right out of his mitts!

After that, I started running to the door. But Meanie Jim springed in front of me. And he held up his hand.

"Stop!" he yelled. "Don't take that valentine outside! If you take it outside, you'll get it dirty."

I made squinty eyes at that boy.

"No, I will not get it dirty," I said back.

"And anyway, this is not your beeswax, Jim."

Jim stamped his foot.

"Yes, it too my beeswax, Looney B. Jones!" he yelled. "That card costed me a whole month's allowance! And I don't want you to get dirt on it!"

As soon as he said it, he quick put his hands over his mouth.

But I already heard his words.

I did a gasp.

"*You*, Jim? You are the one who bought this card?" I asked. "Why? How come? Is this some kind of meanie boy joke?"

Jim started sputtering a real lot.

"Yes. I mean, no. Uh, I mean, I didn't buy that card. It just *looks* like it costed a lot of money, that's all. And whoever bought it spent his whole allowance, I bet."

I kept on staring at that boy. 'Cause something smelled like fish here, that's why.

"But if you're not the one who gave me that valentime, then how come you're acting so funny, Jim?" I asked. "And how come your words are sputtery and nervous? And how come your face is reddish and blotchish?"

Just then, Jim clunked himself in the head.

"Darn it! I *knew* I'd ruin it! I always ruin everything! Now everybody in Room Nine will know that I like you! And I wanted it to stay a secret!" he said.

All of a sudden, my whole face felt happy.

"You *like* me, Jim? You really, really like me? 'Cause you never acted like you like me. And so since when did you like me? That's what I would like to know."

Jim's face got a silly look on it.

"I've always liked you," he said real quiet. "I just *act* like I don't like you, so nobody will know I like you."

I looked confused at him.

"But if you *like* me, how come you always call me names?" I asked.

Jim shrugged his shoulders.

"Because you call *me* names," he said.

I did a big breath.

"Yes, Jim. I *know* I call you names. But that's because you started it first," I explained.

"No, I did not," he said. "*You* started it first."

I shook my head.

"No, Jim. You did," I said.

"No, Junie B. You did," he said back.

"No, *you* did."

"No, *you* did."

"No, *you!*"

All of a sudden, Jim raised his hand in the air. And he waved it all around.

I called on him.

"Jim?" I said.

"Maybe we *both* started it, Junie B.," he said. "Maybe we both started calling each other names on the very same day."

Just then, I started to smile. 'Cause that would be fair of us, I think!

After that, I skipped around him in a happy circle. On account of this was a nice development.

I grabbed his hand.

"Hey, Jim. Let's go tell Mrs. that we're friends. Want to? 'Cause she will get a kick out of this, probably," I said.

But all of a sudden, Jim plopped down on the floor. And he wouldn't even budge.

I stared and stared at the top of his head.

"Okay…this doesn't actually seem like that good of a start for us, Jim," I said.

He looked up at me.

"I know," he said. "But I *can't* tell the teacher that I like you. I can't tell anyone. If I tell people, it will ruin everything."

I wrinkled my eyebrows.

"Everything like what?" I said.

"Like all my friends will know I like girls. And that will be embarrassing," he said. "Plus Room Nine won't ever be the same again."

I didn't understand.

"Why, Jim? Why won't it be the same?" I asked.

"Because it will be dull and boring, that's

why," he said. "Because if you and I like each other, then I won't tease you anymore. And if I don't tease you, then you won't tease me back. And that means you won't shout silly, funny stuff at me that makes people laugh."

He rocked back and forth on his feet very bashful.

"You make Room Nine *sparky*," he said kind of quiet.

After that, he smiled very cute. And he poked my arm with his finger. And he made a sparky sound.

"*Zzzzt!*" he said. "*Zzzzt! Zzzzt!*"

I laughed very loud. And I sparked him right back.

"*Zzzzt! Zzzzt!*" I said.

And so guess what? Then me and that silly guy started chasing each other all over

Room Nine. And we kept poking and sparking! And it was the funnest game I ever even heard of!

Only too bad for us. Because all of a sudden, we heard a noise at the door.

Oh no!

It was Mrs.

She caught us in the room!

"Hey! What's going on in here?" she said. "You two are supposed to be on the playground."

Me and Jim stopped very fast.

Then Jim looked nervous at me. 'Cause he was afraid I would tell his secret, I think.

All of a sudden, I pointed to him kind of mad.

"It's *his* fault, Mrs.," I said. "'Cause Jim poked me and made a sparky sound. And then I had to poke him back and make a sparky sound, too. Only he couldn't let that be the end of it. And so pretty soon we were chasing and sparking, and chasing and sparking. Only just now you came in the door. And so the chasing and sparking are over, apparently. And so we will just be on our way to the playground, I believe."

I tapped on her.

"Pardon me while I get by," I said very polite.

Mrs. rolled her eyes way back in her head.

"Honestly, you two. It's Valentine's Day," she said. "Can't you get along for just one day?"

After that, she took us by our hands. And she marched us outside.

We waited for her to leave.

Then he looked at me kind of shy.

"You did good," he said. "Thank you for not telling my secret."

I smiled at that nice boy.

"That's okay. Thank you for my mushy gushy valentime," I said back.

After that, I faced my eyeball at him.

"Wink, wink, Jim," I said. "Wink, wink, wink."

And guess what?

Jim pointed his eyeball right back at me. And he winked very perfect!

After that, we runned off to play with our friends. Or else people might think we liked each other. And that would ruin everything!

That is how come I never ever told anybody about Jim's secret. Not even my bestest friends, Lucille and Grace.

'Cause Meanie Jim is the bestest secret admirer I ever had.

And guess what else?

Room Nine is still staying sparky!

Zzzzt!

Come visit me
at my very own Web site!

www.randomhouse.com/kids/junieb

Junie B. has a lot to say
about everything and everybody...

the baby's room

Mother and Daddy fixed up a room for the new baby. It's called a nursery. Except I don't know why. Because a baby isn't a nurse, of course.
• from *Junie B. Jones and a Little Monkey Business*

tools

We played a game called Name the Tools. And guess what? I knew the saw. And the hammer. And the metric socket set with adjustable ratchet.
• from *Junie B. Jones and Her Big Fat Mouth*

food preparation

'Greedients is the stuff you mix together. Like the bowl. And the spoon. And the cereal. And the milk.
• from *Junie B. Jones and the Yucky Blucky Fruitcake*

her baby brother

His name is Ollie. I love him a real lot. Except I wish he didn't live at my actual house.
• from *Junie B. Jones and That Meanie Jim's Birthday*